THE PLAGIARIST

BY HUGH HOWEY

The Plagiarist

Copyright © 2011 by Hugh Howey

All rights reserved. No part of this book may be reproduced in any form by any electronic or mechanical means including photocopying, recording, or information storage and retrieval without permission in writing from the author.

ISBN-13: 978-1-460-95819-3
ISBN-10: 1-460-95819-5

www.hughhowey.com

Give feedback on the book at:
hughhowey@hotmail.com

Printed in the U.S.A

For all the great teachers.

1

Adam Griffey lost himself in the familiar glow-in-the-dark sticker. It was a depiction of a bee lighting on a flower, a thirsty proboscis curling out of the insect's cartoony smile. The sticker held Adam's attention. The glow of the bee made it seem radioactive, a poisoned thing. It adorned the edge of his beat-up computer screen, the edges curling away as the sticker lost its grip. The remnants of several other stickers stood idly by, just the bumpy adhesive outlines, the colorful bits having long ago been peeled away by Adam's fidgety hands. He was prone to scratching at them with his fingernails. They weren't his; they came with the old monitor, which he'd bought off another faculty member. Adam figured it belonged to one of their kids, what with the stickers. He thought about that as his eyes fell reluctantly from the bee and back to the screen. There was a message there, a series of messages typed back and forth. They populated a chat window, the only thing open on his screen. The window suddenly blinked with a new question:

lonelyTraveler1: you still there?

Adam picked at the edge of the radioactive bee, thinking of tearing it off. He read back over his conversation with Amanda, his responses in deep blue, hers a bright red. She had asked him a question before he'd gotten distracted. How long had he gone without responding? What would she read in that silence?

His fingers fell to the keyboard, leaving the sticker for another time. He sat motionless, unsure of how to respond. Thoughts whirled. Adam read the second question up. He read it over and over. Where the fuck had it come from? From nowhere, he decided. He had gone too long without reply; he decided to ignore the older question and answer the more recent one:

Griffey575: Yeah. Sorry about that. Doing too much at once.

lonelyTraveler1: you chatting with other people at the same time? you cheating on me? ;)

Adam glanced over the sad and empty expanse of his monitor and laughed to himself. Twenty four inches by twelve inches of pathetic nothingness. His entire social life, his entire *real* romantic life, could be contained in one small chat window in a lonely fraction of that abyss.

Griffey575: I wish.

He typed the response, then held down the backspace key to erase the truth before he could send it.

Griffey575: Work stuff.

He decided that was better. Adam wondered if it counted as a lie if the untruth was as boring as reality.

> lonelyTraveler1: what kinda stuff? for a class you're teaching? are you writing anything? anything you can share?

Adam saw how lies could spawn more lies, each offspring bigger than its parent. The truth was, he'd been neglecting his work and his writing. Possibly, in no small part, because of Amanda's constant badgering to read more. She was—if not his online girlfriend—at least his anti-muse, the woman whose insistence quenched all motivation. Adam had known this of himself since he was an undergrad: he couldn't think when being told to.

> lonelyTraveler1: you still haven't answered my other question...

Which one? Adam thought.

> Griffey575: Which one?

He hit enter before he could regret asking. He knew which question. He didn't want to know, but he did. His stomach lurched with the audaciousness of her suggestion. And what did that say about him? How could he have a fake relationship with the real, and a real one with the fake? Which relationship was *more* real? Which was sicker? And who was the victim? Was anyone really being betrayed?

> lonelyTraveler1: don't you think it's time we meet up?

There it was again. It was crazy.

Griffey575: In person?

lonelyTraveler1: how else?

Adam watched the cursor blink where he was expected to respond. The glowing bee radiated stored sunlight in his peripheral. In the utter darkness around him, he sensed the piles of clutter everywhere. He kept meaning to get to it. He kept the lights off in his apartment, kept the blinds drawn, so he couldn't see the reminders of his laziness. The bee dimly betrayed him with its steady glow.

Griffey575: This way seems nice.

After the barest of pauses, he added a smiley face:

Griffey575: :)

It wasn't sarcasm. It wasn't real humor. It was an apology, something to soften the blow of what he knew to be the wrong answer. Adam had replied incorrectly; Amanda's silence confirmed it. An icon came up to let him know she was typing something. It disappeared for a moment, reappeared, then disappeared again. He was watching her think. He wondered what things had been erased, if it was anger or disappointment she was refraining from sending.

Griffey575: I think I'm just not ready.

He wondered if that sounded better. It at least filled the silence.

lonelyTraveler1: I'm gonna find out you're married, aren't I?

Griffey575: I'm not married.

Such lies were not in him. Such a life, perhaps, was not in him.

lonelyTraveler1: but there's someone else.

Griffey575: There's no person else.

Clumsy. The sentence sounded stilted, but it kept his response, strictly speaking, from being an outright lie.

lonelyTraveler1: I won't push you. just think about it. or at least write me something, write me something about why you'd want to or not want to.

A pause.

lonelyTraveler1: I feel like we're living in 2 separate worlds lately.

Adam laughed nervously. His fingers left the keyboard and moved to rub his sore temples. For a brief moment, just an insane instant, he considered telling Amanda the truth. He pictured typing all the craziness of his life out in one uninterrupted, suicidal message. He imagined her sitting there, staring at the icon that let her know he was typing for hours and hours while he crafted a biopic admission of how scary and surreal and demented his life had become…

He deleted the thought.

Griffey575: I do have a piece I haven't shared.

His mind was suddenly in a spilling mood—as long as it was spilling *other* things. It sought release of some cryptic truth. There were thousands of haikus that Adam kept to himself. They lived in his head, swirling beneath the layered façades, keeping him company. The impulse to let one out became great. He figured he could trade it for the impossible thing Amanda was asking, this meeting each other in person. Perhaps a bartered poem could delay the inevitable.

lonelyTraveler1: oh. PLEASE!!

Griffey575: Just one, then I really need to get some sleep. I have an early class.

lonelyTraveler1: is this a new one? when did you write it?

When did he write it? He couldn't exactly remember. All his life, Adam had wanted to be a writer. The problem was: he was too good at *reading*. He had too many of Shakespeare's sonnets memorized. Too much Blake and Shelly and Proust. All that good stuff was crammed up in his brainstem, pooled in his pons, dripping down his spine, now a part of his very fiber. Trying to sneak a sham of his own past such a gang of real McCoys was impossible. Adam's great gift—knowing the good stuff—was also his failing. The only words of his own that he could sneak through his literature-stuffed brain were his little haikus, unassuming and light on their feet. They were like neutrinos streaming out from the dense center of a star, cruising across the cosmos invisible and unknowable.

> Griffey575: About a year ago I think.

He hit enter, let the words come to him from memory.

> Griffey575: Here it goes; then I need to get away from this screen:
>
> > Moments spill through hands
> > idling away at nothing
> > To puddle in years

 Adam logged off, but the chat window remained open. It held another uncomfortable conversation he could scroll through and regret. He read over the poem and realized that at that very moment, Amanda was reading it as well. They were both *seeing* it for the first time. It was as if some part of him had been excised. Released. Set free and exposed.

 He wondered how much of him she would see in the poem. Could it be read in any way other than the obvious? Full of regrets? A loser continuing to lose?

 Not for the first time, he tried to imagine what Amanda looked like. Not that it mattered, but the human brain seemed to need to know. Eyes were used to engaging with other eyes while voices crossed. They were too accustomed to scanning faces for revealing twitches, the curl of lips, the flare of nostrils. Speaking in nothing but font was unnatural and stifling.

Adam gave the webcam above the psychedelic bee a nervous glance. It wasn't plugged in, never had been; it came with the monitor. Still, it felt like people could see him sometimes, see the real him stripped of his avatars. Not Amanda, not his mother or sister or anyone he knew—he felt like millions of *strangers* could see him in his dark and filthy room, like they spent hours watching him, like they knew him better than he knew himself.

Adam closed the chat window, turned off his computer, rubbed his eyes. It was so late it was early. And Amanda had been right, even if she'd only meant it as a figure of speech: they *were* spending too much time on different planets. The haiku, he thought, captured that all too well. So much simplicity and truth in seventeen syllables. And now it was out in the world and no longer rattling around in his brain. He laughed to himself, scratched the beard sneaking out of his skin, then saw the hour and realized he had the time for neither a nap nor shower. Not if he was going to see his other girlfriend before his eight o'clock class.

2

> Between these temples,
> aching and burning and sore
> my universe lies

He only had two hours before he had to be at class, but the simulator would make it feel like six. Blazing computer chips worked much like morning dreams, compressing time. It made living two lives all that easier.

Adam used his faculty pass to swipe his way to the labs, then picked one of the jacks in the far corner. He had the room to himself, four in the morning being too late for most and too early for all, but he still went for as much privacy as possible, knowing he would probably have company before he jacked out. There were only a few reasons to hit the sims at certain times of the day, prostitution being the foremost. Adam wished the stigma weren't true in his case. He wished.

The seat squeaked as he settled into it. Adam swiped his ID through the reader; the beeps and whirrings of the booting machine were as familiar as a favorite song. And like music, they did something to his autonomic nervous system: his sleepless brain felt a jolt of energy, a dangerous surge of love and lust. He took his temple pads from his backpack, untangled them from each other, then wiped the cups off on his shirt. A dab of adhesive grease went on each, then he pressed them to the sore points on either side of his head—points he could feel without having to check the mirror. The burn there had become constant.

Adam waited impatiently for the simulation to boot. This was the longest part of his day. He could compress all the rest of his hours right into these handful of moments, he was sure. It was also the time when he truly reflected on what he had become, what he was about to do. It was in these moments that he truly loathed himself.

The lab disappeared as the sim took hold. The twinkling lights of the idling machines all around him were replaced by alien constellations. Adam floated in the center of an artificial cosmos. He was God. He could go to any dozens of planets and planetary nebula, observe tectonic plates shifting with x-ray vision, or zoom to the level of the protein and watch the molecules fold as salinity and temperature shifted. His choices were limitless, but of course he had no choice. He hurriedly selected a familiar star out of one of the constellations. The star was named Beatrice Bondeamu Gilbert III, after the donor who paid for the servers on which it was hosted. Artificial stars were like academic halls: a few million dollars and your name lived on forever.

He aimed for the fourth planet out from the star, nestled right in the Goldilocks zone. The glowing blue-green ball was named Hammond after Beatrice's late husband. Adam "chose" the planet with his mind. It was as simple as looking at something and wanting it. He wanted it.

There were a million ways to approach the planet. If from the entomology department, one might swoop through the night clouds like a bat, virtual sonar picking up invisible bugs to collect. The climatologists would play like gods bored with their food, sitting over the clouds and swirling them with their fingers, taking notes, testing theories. Geneticists would become the size of molecules and be lost in worlds the scope of Mendelian peas, causing mutations. Adam had little use for such scientific probings. He remained much as himself, if a little taller, thicker of hair, more tan, and less paunchy. His virtual being emerged from a bathroom stall in a bookstore he had claimed as his own territory—had paid quite well for it, in fact. He pushed open the door and nodded to a customer walking by.

Hammond was one of the handful of humanoid planets, where evolution had been rigged to emulate Earth's. As such, it was not as jarring to be an avatar as some xeno-sims could be. It felt perfectly natural to nod to someone who didn't exist, who was just a bunch of ones and zeros. The computer simulated customer smiled and nodded in return. It, of course, thought it was real. The customer thought the book it was about to pick up and peruse was real. It thought the sunshine streaming through the front windows, and the grime streaked across those windows, and the dust floating in the air like a grid of stars, and the clatter of bells whacked by an opening door—every simulated person in the entire bookstore thought every single bit of it, including themselves, was all real.

Adam soaked it in. He wanted it to be real as well.

"Hey!"

He turned. Belatrix stood behind him, her green work apron hanging around her neck, two creases running down it vertically from having been meticulously folded the night before. Curls of brown hair hung like springs behind her ears. Her bright eyes smiled at him, crinkles radiating away from their corners. "I didn't see you come in," she said. At least, that's how it was translated for Adam.

Belatrix showed him the small stack of books she was shelving, as if to apologize for not hugging him. Adam smiled what he knew to be a perfectly symmetrical smile full of brilliant teeth.

"I kinda snuck past to the bathroom." He waved a little wave to forgive the lack of a hug. Adam glanced at the books in her hands. "You getting off soon?"

"I am."

She was. Adam knew she was. He had chosen the time carefully when he logged in. He had to be in class in two hours, but the flow rate would give him six. Belatrix smiled at him then slid a book into place. Adam tried not to think of the *other* him, the fleshy him, and the *real* world waiting and spinning around him. He gave himself up completely to the sim.

"How was work?" Belatrix asked as she pushed open her apartment door and shrugged off her coat. It had drizzled on their walk over from the bookstore. Adam wiped his feet on her mat, then kicked off his shoes. Details like the mud, the shiny drops of water on the tile—he still marveled at the completeness of the illusion, the scope and scale of the digitally constructed world. It was easy to lose oneself in it, to become bewildered by it all.

"That interesting, huh?"

Adam broke out of his trance and helped Belatrix hang her jacket on the hook by the door. "Work was fine," he said. "Closed a pretty big deal this week."

He was sure it was true. When he wasn't present to fill and steer his avatar, the computers moved it about as autonomously as anyone else on planet Hammond. Belatrix, in fact, had probably spent more time in his avatar's place of work than he had.

"Some tea?"

"Sure," he said, even though he hated the stuff. It wasn't tea, but that was the closest translation for the language parser. Horseshit would have been more apt, but the translator stuck to categories such as "warm beverages." The only thing it left untouched were proper nouns, which left Adam's avatar with the moniker of Phurxy, a dreadfully common name on Hummond's Southwest continent.

"Bitter apple?" Belatrix held up a grainy lump of spice. Again, the translation was a mere approximation.

"Please," Adam said. It made the hot horseshit taste more like wet dirt, a distinct improvement. Adam often considered fast flowing the time through these bits, but the domestic foreplay was a crucial part of the fantasy. *This* was the life he wanted to live, here with Belatrix in her tidy apartment. He took the steaming bowl and glanced in the mirror at his clean and neatly groomed self. His avatar had taken the time to do that in the morning, brushing his teeth *and* his hair. It felt like room service for the body and soul. He luxuriated in his sense of self.

"*Seamonsters and Mist* is opening up at the cinema this weekend." Belatrix took a loud sip and looked at him over the rim of her bowl. "You wanna go see it?"

"Love to," he said. It felt amazing to make plans for his avatar's time, knowing he wouldn't have to go—but that he would. He drank as much wet dirt as he could take, set the bowl aside, then plopped down on one of the floor cushions. "I'm feeling kinda horny," he said with a grin.

Belatrix smiled and set aside her bowl.

Adam could get away with saying such forward things—he could rush the moment with her—because he didn't do it often.

He did it every time.

3

> Even these false worlds
> with their oceans and vast plains
> can't hold all my lies

Adam arrived late to his eight o'clock class. His students were already there, sitting like powered down robots, gazing ahead, awaiting commands from him. He closed the door—too loudly—and felt annoyed by the quiet. He would've preferred the film cliché: balled paper flying; kids sitting on desks swinging their feet; boys with bravado and girls with batting lashes twisting in their seats. In all his years of teaching, he'd never seen such a scene, not once. It was always the blank stares, the lethargy, the sense among them that the first who moved or uttered a word would be eaten by the others—or worse, be made unpopular.

Adam dumped a stack of papers on his desk and made a show of arranging them, anything to disturb the thick silence of the room. He resented his eight o'clock class. He knew they felt the same way, but what were they missing? More sleep? Escape from their hangovers? He was missing an entire other life he preferred to live, a life that was daily truncated by a day job he wished he didn't need. He thought this as he scanned their faces, all a weird mix of wide eyes and boredom. If it weren't for the access to the University server farms and their sims, he wouldn't put up with the kids at all. Well, the sims and the health care. The health care was nice.

He shuffled papers around and tried to glean from graded assignments which class this was. He had nothing planned for the day. He rarely did of late.

The hypocrisy of Adam's new existence, the layers and layers of hypocrisy, were always right at the surface, staring back at him. He had become a master of procrastination. Like the students he had long mocked, he had honed the art of putting things off until they were simply never done. He lived under a heavy blanket of shirked responsibilities; they weighed on him every moment, this great pile of many things that needed to be done. He no longer knew where to start. It was all about getting through each moment, getting through the day to enjoy the nights, faking his real life so he could live his fake one.

More hypocrisy: Adam used to mock his kids for their addiction to video games—now he lived in one of his own. He remembered his disgust at virtual marriages between players who had never met, stories about trolls and paladins exchanging digital vows. Now he had one girlfriend he had never met, and he discussed marriage and kids with another person who didn't really exist.

Then there was the plagiarism—his greatest hypocrisy of them all.

"Does somebody want to pass these out?" Adam gathered up the graded assignments and waved them with one hand. He hadn't actually taken the time to read them, just verified that they existed. A student he particularly loathed, seated to Adam's left, was the first to volunteer. The boy took the papers eagerly. Adam rubbed his palms over his eyes and his fingers through his unwashed hair. The plagiarism was his greatest hypocrisy by far. If any of his students plagiarized, they would be flunked. They knew that from the start. It was the greatest sin as a student, as a thinker, and it was a temptation they struggled to avoid. Adam, meanwhile, did it for a *living*. His second job, the one that paid most of his bills, was to steal the words of others. But lately he hadn't even been able to summon the motivation to do that. While the papers, marked with their red checks and little else, fluttered their way through the room, an old conversation with his mother came back to Adam. He remembered the first time he had tried to explain his new vocation, and how unimpressed she had been.

****

"I'm just so proud of you honey!"

"Thanks, Mom." Adam held the phone under his chin, the speaker angled away from his face. The extra distance dampened the ear-splitting scream of his mother's voice, who seemed to think her words needed extra force to cross the two time zones between them.

"My own son, an author." Adam could picture her gingerly lifting each page of the book as she skimmed through it. "Cindy from my bridge club bought a copy. We're racing each other to the end, but not so fast I can't enjoy it."

"That's great, Mom, but you do know—"

"I really love the Marsha character. When she tells Reginold to get out of his own house—"

"Hey, Ma?"

"I love that part. Yes, Dear?"

"You're not telling people that I wrote the book are you?" Adam nuzzled the phone against his ear and pulled on the silence. He could hear his mother's exhalations on the other end, breathless from excitement. He didn't call as often as he should.

"Your name is on the cover," she said. "Adam Griffey. And you dedicated it to your mom. That's me."

"Mom, I *discovered* the book. We've talked about this. It says it right there with the copyrights."

"But this is your book." The pain in her voice was gut wrenching.

"Yes, and the royalties are mine, and I get a lot of credit with some people for discovering it, but it wasn't written by me. Please don't tell Cindy or any of your other friends that I wrote the book. I don't want to have to explain it on holidays—"

"So who wrote it?" Her voice had gone quiet. Adam could hear her flipping through pages, could almost picture her weathered fingers quivering as she did so. He had told her about this. He remembered telling her about this.

"Mom, do you remember the worlds I told you about? The simulated ones where people here at the university study the weather, and the way the plates of the crust move, and how stars and moons form and all that?"

"The video games?"

Adam sighed. He looked from a pile of dirty laundry

to a moldy mound of stacked plastic dishes rising out of the sink. He had none of the time for this.

"It's similar to video games, Mom, but a lot more complex and a lot more useful. People do real good research in there. That cure for testicular cancer that's been all over the news? It came from one of these worlds."

"They cure cancer there?"

Adam felt like he was teaching his mother to perform brain surgery over the phone. *Keep your index finger extended along the back of the scalpel, like so, but a little bent. You've got the cordless drill charged up? Make the first incision—*

"They do a lot of things on these worlds, Ma. They're a lot like *this* world. People get up and drive to work. It rains and things get wet. They erect buildings, and the windows need washing after a while. And people write books and plays and poetry and what-not."

"And someone on this world wrote this book?"

"Yeah."

"And you just took it?"

"Ma, you know these people aren't real, right?"

"So they don't mind? Do you tell them?"

"No we don't—" Adam thought about it. They *would* mind, wouldn't they? "Mom, we can't exactly tell them that they aren't real, that we created them and we really like their work so we're gonna share it in the real world."

"Why not?" His mother grunted, sounding disgusted with him. "I thought I raised you better."

Adam slapped his palm on his chest. "It isn't up to *me*, Ma! I don't make the rules. Besides, I don't think you could convince these people. They think they're just as real as you and me. They'd probably lock you up in a padded room until you logged off."

"Logged off—?"

"Forget it, Ma."

"What am I supposed to tell my friends?"

"Tell them I'm really good at what I do. Tell them that I can memorize fifteen pages in a single session, word for word. Tell them there's no way we can copy stuff straight out of the quantum drives, Mom. Say that. Tell them "quantum drives." Tell them that there's hundreds of thousands of people trying to do what I do, to find that one great work of art in a sea of tripe, and most of them can't. Tell your friends that I'm really good at seeing the true genius among the piles of plain stories. Tell them that *I'll* be the one to find the next Shakespeare, Mom."

"But you won't tell him?"

"Tell who?"

"This new Shakespeare. You'll memorize his stuff, and you won't tell him."

Adam cradled the phone to his ear and let out his breath. "He wouldn't believe me, Ma, even if I did. These people aren't real. It's like a video game, just like you said."

"So Marsha and Reginold—"

"Those are characters in a book written by a virtual person." Adam said it slowly.

"But they're in love with each other."

He sighed. "I suppose they are. In their own weird way."

"How did a video game write about that?"

"Hey, Ma? I gotta go. I've got a class in an hour."

"Does your girlfriend, does Amanda know this is what you do?"

"Yeah," Adam lied.

"And she's okay with it?"
"Of course." He rubbed his temples.
"When am I going to meet her?"
Not before I do, Adam thought.
"Soon," he said.
"Okay. Well, I still like the book."
"Thanks, Ma."
"Even if you did steal it from some poor person."

4

> The ones and zeros
> like snow, descend and blanket
> my eyes, forming all.

Adam patted his pockets as he left his apartment, making sure he had his keys. It was winter; the days were short. A blanket of black hung over the campus, and a blanket of white covered the ground. He shut the apartment door too hard, rattling the windows. Of late, all doors seemed to close too hard for him or not at all. They were slammed or left wanting. It was about motor control, and Adam was losing his. He looked back to the shuddering window and saw his reflection. The scruff on his jaw measured the long nights, nights such as these when he should sleep but couldn't. Despite his fatigue, he remained awake, a diurnal creature in the opposite of day.

"Griff?"

Adam turned to find his friend standing at the bottom of his apartment's stoop, freshly falling snow gathering on his knit cap like stars shaken from the darkness overhead.

"Hey, Samualson."

"You ready?" Samualson asked. He had a look of concern on his face, a look Adam was getting used to seeing. His friend was a decade older than him and half a foot taller. A neatly trimmed beard and fitted coat lent him a professorial look. He seemed more the English scholar than Adam felt, even though he was a member of the hard sciences. The two of them had become friends after seeing each other in the labs every night. They found there was something less pathetic about coming and going to the sims with another *real* person.

Adam shrugged his bookbag over his shoulder and followed Samualson down the walk. The campus arranged across the valley below was illuminated by tall night lights and the sliver of a waning moon. The snow on the ground and in the air seemed to gather and magnify the light. The shallow impressions of footsteps littered the ground, already half full again with falling snow. Adam hurried up beside Samualson, their boots crunching and squeaking in the wet pack.

"Hey, did you hear?" Thick smoke streamed out with Samualson's voice, the moisture of his breath crystalized in the cold night air.

"Did I hear?" Adam tugged his gloves on and patted them together. "Did I hear what? I hear tons. I hear too much."

"Virginia Tech." Samualson turned his head as a gust of wind brought cold and a flurry of blown snow. "Their farm got razed."

"Razed? As in gone?"

"Every single server got deleted. Formatted."

"You're shittin' me." Adam tucked his scarf into his collar. "When? Last night? Today?" He couldn't believe he hadn't heard.

Samualson groped in a pocket and drew out an orb of light, the glow of his phone dazzling the snow. "Just now." He flashed the screen at Adam. "Read about it on the walk over. They think the Writer's Guild might be responsible, but again, nobody's taking credit."

Adam shook his head. "How are they doing this? That's three farms wiped out this month."

"Yeah." They turned a corner around the administration building, entering its lee and escaping the bitter wind. "Three farms went online this month and three others got hosed. That's pretty weird."

Adam's exhalations billowed in the air in front of him before trailing off behind. He pulled his scarf over his mouth. "How many worlds was Tech simming?" His voice was muffled and wet against his nose.

"Sixteen. Four Humanoid and the rest Xeno. I work with a guy who had remote access to some of them. He's gonna be crushed. Was in the middle of some good research there."

"Sixteen worlds. Fuck me, that's a lot to lose." Adam glanced up at the sliver of a moon hanging over campus.

"They're saying something close to eighty billion sentients are gone. No telling how many lesser critters."

"Or works of art," Adam reminded him.

Samualson shrugged and stuffed his phone away. His hands were pale blue from the cold. He dug in another pocket and pulled a pair of gloves out, then wiggled them on. "That's your domain," he said.

They shuffled in near silence across the campus. Adam could hear the tinkle of invisible sleet hitting the crust of snow around him. It was a small campus, which kept the jaunts short, but it was hilly and prone to gasping and wheezing. The university was kept small by necessity, nestled down and crowded in by three rising slopes, like two bosoms and a great belly, all perched on the thin sternum of a high mountain valley. It was a place that caught snow and gathered high-flying and lost souls. Griffey considered that as they reached the Madison Mitchell Jr. Computer Science building. He stamped snow off his boots while Samualson fumbled through his ring of keys. Adam watched a snowflake fall on the back of his glove, the white standing out on the black for a moment before the edges of the fragile crystalline structure folded up into a drop of water. The clarity of the transformation was stunning.

"Look how real all this is," he said aloud, not meaning to.

Samualson turned and studied his friend, a shiny key pinched between the padded fingers of his glove.

"You feeling okay? You look like shit, man."

Adam glanced up from the falling, melting stars. "How does it feel this real when we're in there?" He jerked his head up at the building. Samualson turned back to the lock, inserted the key and opened the door, which squealed on frozen hinges.

"I take it you don't dream much."

Adam laughed and stomped snow off his boots. "I don't even *sleep* much anymore."

"Well if you slept more, you'd dream more, and you'd see how good your brain is at making something out of nothing." He held the door open for Adam, who shuffled through, followed by a dusting of snow. "You know there's a spot in the center of your vision where you can't see, right?"

"Where the retina goes through." Adam nodded. He didn't see the connection.

"Your brain fills in that blank spot perfectly." The door clanged shut behind them. "I was talking to a professor in the bio department about this a month ago. You know what he said? He said roughly thirty percent of everything we see is hallucination. It's our brain smoothing things over so the world's not so *pixelated*." Samualson nodded down the hallway. "That's how everything in there feels just as real as this, as real as our dreams." He patted Adam on the back, letting loose a small avalanche of clinging snow. "Seriously, man, you've gotta get some sleep. Why don't you take a night or two off? These worlds aren't going anywhere."

"That's what Virginia Tech thought."

Samualson laughed. "Ours are a pittance compared to that. Nobody's gunning for us."

Adam shrugged, and the two of them fell silent save for the squeak of their wet boots. He imagined—or hallucinated—that he could hear the collective roar of billions of tiny whispering, virtual souls as they approached the interface room. He thought about the server farm nearby with its tall cabinets of computer equipment adorned with blinking lights. Hundreds of busy little mechanical arms clicked back and forth somewhere inside the quantum hard drives, like the arms of miniature gods waving over a dozen digitized worlds, creating and destroying all the time.

5

> The connected few.
> Billions of neurons and souls.
> So few connected.

The interface room was packed. Adam had rarely seen it so full during a night shift. Usually they would find a lone professor or technician in the room working late. Adam preferred it like that, preferred it more when he had the place to himself. He worried his facial twitches or some uttered word would give away his romantic trysts. He'd never gleaned anything from Samualson that made Adam think his friend suspected, but still he worried. The two of them often mocked those who jacked in to jack off. It was no secret lots of professors did. Regular porn had nothing on virtual whores who didn't even know they were virtual, and tenure had been revoked over particularly exotic sprees. Adam justified what he did because he was in love, or thought he was.

"Damn," Samualson said, seeing the crowd. "Is there a rally tonight?" He glanced over at the scheduling board where groups signed out clusters of terminals for virtual meetings. One of the bigger groups on campus was the cycling club, a habit more loathsome than jerking off in Adam's opinion. These people actually simmed bicycle riding. They spent their time on foreign worlds, riding bikes, their brains flooded with endorphins from simulated exhaustion. Adam could always sense when he was interfacing right after a cyclist. The seat would remain warm for hours, the stench of sleep-sweat in the air. It was disgusting. The fact that most of them were grossly overweight didn't help.

"There's two over in that corner," Samualson said.

Adam flipped his backpack around and dug for his temple patches. He followed his friend through the busy room.

"What're you searching after tonight?" Samualson asked. He sat down in front of one of the terminals and squeezed gel from a tube and onto his finger. "That elusive Shakespeare?"

Adam laughed. "I've given up on finding him." He plugged his temple patches into a pair of cords dangling from outlets on the wall. "There'll never be another Bard of Avon."

"That children's series you picked up last year seems to be doing pretty well." He dabbed gel onto his temples, checking the placement in the small circular mirror mounted on the wall in front of him. Adam did the same; they looked like performers getting ready for a show, an apt illusion.

"That series is drivel," Adam said. He smiled at his friend's reflection. "Don't get me wrong, the royalties are good, but I'd rather have the hours back I spent memorizing them."

"Or the brain cells."

Both men laughed as they began pressing the interface pads into the dabs of gel. Adam tried to ignore the blue crescents under his eyes as he secured the connection. Sleep had become as virtual, as ephemeral, as his work.

"So whatcha after, then?" Samualson wouldn't leave the line of questioning alone. The machines at their feet hummed to life, leaving thick seconds to fill with banter.

"I'm dabbling in art, actually." He glanced at Samualson and hoped the shame of the lie would adequately mimic the shame of the truth he was hiding.

"Art?" His friend chuckled softly as he pressed the pads to his temples. "Good luck with that."

"It's all luck," Adam admitted. "Are you still working on that same protein?"

Samualson flipped open a pad of paper and touched a pen to his tongue, a nervous tic more than a functional act. The woman interfaced on the other side of him twitched, her head leaping up from her folded arms then crashing back down again. "Yup," Samualson said. He slid pages up the spiral bound pad to find his place. Adam saw line after line of four letters repeated: CTTGACATGCA… It seemed like mind-numbing work. He imagined his friend peering into a virtual microscope, or cyclotron, or whatever biologists used, and memorizing a few hundred letters at a time—jacking out—writing them down—jacking back in. It gave Adam a headache just thinking about it and made him appreciate his own work. If they transcribed a few letters the wrong way, a cure for liver cancer might instead turn a poor kid into a glow stick. If Adam got a word or two wrong, nobody knew or really cared. Unlike his brief haiku, the sheer mass of a full length piece of writing could absorb a handful of mistakes.

The machine at Adam's feet beeped, letting him know he had a connection to the school's server farm. Adam liked that it was called a "farm." He smiled at the thought of worlds springing up from plowed rows of dirt, cloud-like shrouds unwrapping to reveal blue and spiral-green planets of life. The word farm, of course, was a holdover from the clusters of computers, the server farms, used at places like Pixar, where virtual worlds were created for entertainment. It took a while before the productive uses of such worlds were understood. Once they were, the result was often referred to as the third great agricultural revolution. Sim farms, in just the last decade, had sprouted all over the place. Government owned, university owned, even a few private ones. The flood of research from these farms drowned out all the work done in the real world. A theory would be published in the morning and overturned by mid-afternoon. Planetary formation and plate tectonics; punctuated equilibrium and mass extinctions; arsenic-based lifeforms and exoskeletons. If you weren't jacked in, you weren't playing.

Science became exciting again overnight. It moved to the forefront much like the days of the great space race in the previous century. Everyone wanted the red blisters on their temples from too much virtual time— the badges of important work being made. Universities and even high schools changed tack overnight, catering to the surge in computer science and math majors. The hard stuff dominated the soft sciences, and the liberal arts soon clamored for a place on campus. This scientific renaissance lasted three years—and then there was Dylan Pyle to restore order.

Adam's temples began to heat up as the interface computer booted. His thoughts turned to Dylan Pyle as the connection took hold.

Eight years ago, nobody had ever heard of Dylan, nor should they have ever. A biology research assistant with dim prospects, Dylan transformed overnight into the greatest living author of all time. His debut novel, *Whispering to Ghosts*, won every award it qualified for, and some that were marginal. He followed it up with a crime novel that re-wrote all the rules, and then came a young adult tome as successful as it was massive. The only thing more surprising than this young man's mix of prolificacy and talent was his refusal to take his writing career seriously. "I dabble," he would say in rare interviews. "I'm a scribbler, nothing more." The reticence to accept his talent, the reclusiveness, the desire to stay on as a humble research assistant, to pour himself into his lab work, it all served to heighten his fame. The glass bubble around him survived three years of awe and praise. It shattered when a fellow researcher discovered Dylan's secret: the boy had a single talent, one of near-photographic memory. He was found in one of his research worlds reading a novel in a park and committing the prose to memory. Selecting from the top writers of several worlds, he had translated their genius into his own, word for word, colon for colon.

Adam felt a tingle at the base of his skull, then a buzz like electric zippers pulling back over his crown; his skull seemed to split in half. He shivered with the out-of-body experience, the sense of his *self* floating out the top of his head before it was sucked back into his gut. He grunted, heard an utterance by Samualson get cut off by the transfer, and then he was gone. He was joining the legions of plagiarists who had followed in Dylan Pyle's wake, soaring down to artificial worlds, scraping them dry of their great art before the scientists were otherwise done with them.

There should have been an uproar, Adam thought. There should have been controversy over what Pyle had done. There should have been outrage. Those would have been normal human responses to having been duped. But a stronger impulse seized the popular imagination: the ability to be great *overnight*. It was a new type of lottery, one where fame and talent were won rather than simple money. The heyday of the sciences came to a sudden close. Discoveries were still made, of course. Real progress was won in astrophysics, biology, psychology, and other fields. But suddenly, the science wings and computer science centers were overrun with talentless hipsters who thought they had an eye for genius. Courses on memorization were invented. Adderall replaced coffee as the recreational drug of choice. Server farms groaned under the stress. Temples were seared. Tubes of adhesive gel were rolled dry.

The *Anti*-Renaissance ensued. As Adam logged into his account, he shivered at the memory of it. Hell, he was still living it. The outpouring of *stuff*, of *crap*, was so intense, nothing could be seen or heard. The variety and quantity were too much. It was a repeat of what YouFilm did to cinema, what AutoTune did to the music industry, what genetic splicing had done to sports. The bar wasn't raised so much as buried under the pile of crap.

And offline talent, *actual* talent, rebelled. Farms were attacked, physically, by supposed bands of marginal musicians and writers. The artists and the avant garde became the new bomb-chuckers. And meanwhile, consumers were pulling away from it all, paralyzed by the sudden confusion of too much choice and novelty. Entire industries suffered.

The interface lab fully dissolved, and an entire universe of simmed worlds appeared before Adam. Here is where he would've, a year ago, agonized over the choices available to him. So many worlds full of so many pages of written words, all of them open to his perusal. But it had been a long time since he'd really chosen. He was now more an automaton than the sims he lived among. He moved his virtual self, shifted his awareness, and went to select the planet where his loved one resided—

And that's when Adam Griffey saw the deletion notice hovering above the planet.

6

> It may be erased,
> all that is written. Destroyed,
> all that's created.

The deletion notice loomed massive over Hammond. Large white numbers on a red background flicked as they slowly counted down the planet's final moments. Adam felt his real stomach drop, back on Earth. He felt all the emotions of shock and rage and sadness, even as he floated bodiless through the void. His plans for the night were over. His plans for the week were over. He didn't have any plans else. Adam's existence had suddenly become as vapid as this simulated consciousness in the black. He was death.

As he floated closer to the planet, he saw that there were just over two hours left, sim time. Two hours for Belatrix to live and breathe. Two hours for him to do nothing for her. It was around eleven thirty when he'd logged on, so the deletion must be slated for midnight, Earth time. The end of the day. The end of *all* days for the people of Hammond.

Adam had a sudden and strange urge to log out and tell Samualson, to let him know that *this* was the reason for the packed interface room. It was Hammond. He imagined the remote access groups would be going nuts as well, logging on from universities and access points all over Earth. It would be a free-for-all, grabbing what data they could, performing wild experiments that would break the suspension of disbelief for the planet's inhabitants. Adam had watched from a distance once while meteors rained down on a planet where lived some decent playwrights. He hadn't even had time to finish memorizing a work he'd been in the middle of, one with quite a bit of potential. That play took up half a notebook in his apartment; the too-hopeful idea was that he'd finish it himself one day.

Despondent and not knowing what to do, Adam drilled into the countdown's menu to look for the slated reason for the planet's deletion. It made no sense to log off and tell Samualson; his friend would see for himself, or he'd find out later. Besides, he suspected there was some other reason he wanted to log off. He felt as if he were dangerously close to coming clean about his affair. He had the urge to make Belatrix real by dragging her name back to his planet; he wanted to yell and scream at someone to not do it, to call off the erasure.

Adam felt all this—he felt anxious and desperate as he continued to drift ever nearer to Hammond. The truth of it began to fully set in. The woman he loved, virtual or not, would cease to exist in two hours. She'd be gone forever. She had been diagnosed with something terminal and sudden.

Adam read the deletion report:

> With the advent of their own simmed worlds, planet Hammond has placed undue stress on our server farms. Planetology research will be suspended, to be resumed once the world re-accretes around the star Beatrice Bondeamu Gilbert III, as per the Astronomy department's request. All sociological studies will be terminated forthwith. Deletion is slated for midnight, February 21st, 2022.

Adam's dimensionless body sped past the message, his mind absorbing it numbly as he went. Why did they have to delete the entire planet? Why not destroy the server farms on Hammond? Why not just delete those? They can rebuild a planet, but not the people. The people would be different. Their writing would be different. Their food and names and language would be different. Their bookstores and the people who worked there would be different.

Adam didn't want different.

He slid into his usual avatar with the shiver of numbness turning to sensation, like new skin pulled over unfeeling muscle. The clouds of Hammond parted as Adam chose his arrival destination; bright sunlight winked out, replaced by the dark interior of the bookstore's bathroom. Adam fumbled for the light, then the doorknob. They were in the same place as before, but it took him a moment. He had become uncentered from himself. As he stepped out into the smell of fresh pulp and horseshit tea, the tiled floor below him seemed closer than it should be. His mind was spinning; he wondered what he would say, what he was even doing here. His shameful and wonderful trysts were over. His love was gone. He wouldn't have to think of anything to tell his mother. He wouldn't have to worry about his father spinning in his grave, or his sister finding out and being humiliated for him. He didn't have to lie to Amanda or Samualson. He didn't have to burn with embarrassment under the unknowing glare of his students.

As he weaved through the stacks of books, Adam became dizzy with all the implications and outcomes. He wanted none of it, not even the relief from this burden. He would gladly lie for another year, another month, another week, just one more day. At least a full day to process it. A day to sit in the park with Belatrix and break the news, maybe even let her think he was crazy. There was so much of her world she had never seen, places Adam had flown over, invisible, and wanted to take her. He hurried down the line of registers, looking for her. She wasn't there. Where were the customers? There was a commotion outside. Adam looked past the displays of bestsellers, through the glass, and saw that the cars in the street were at a standstill. Horns blared in the distance. Someone was screaming, the voice muted. Adam whirled around and realized he was the only one in the store. Him and a single cashier, who was emptying the register and stuffing his pants. Adam didn't recognize him; he was pretty sure he didn't work there.

"Where is everyone?" Adam asked the man.

"Fuck off! These are mine."

The man moved to another register and began pounding buttons. Fans of colorful bills flopped above his belt. A car roared outside, pulled up on the sidewalk and rumbled by, scattering screaming pedestrians. Adam watched it squeal out of sight, then he pushed the glass doors open and hurried outside.

"There's another one!" someone screamed. The crowd moved as one, heads turning to follow an angled arm and a pointing finger. Eyes were shielded against the midday glare. Adam turned and looked up as well. A massive flying saucer rumbled overhead, ridiculous lights splaying out of it. The thunder of explosions grumbled in the distance, sending shivers of panic through the crowd. Adam couldn't believe it. Of all the sociological experiments to level on the Southwest continent, an alien invasion had to be the dumbest he could think of. What was the point? How had this request won out? Unless it was for some professor's amusement. He pushed his way through the crowd toward Belatrix's apartment, thankful they hadn't picked a flood or meteor impact for the area. He spotted a few other researchers in the crowd, their remote access icons blinking visibly—to Adam at least—above their heads. One icon sported University of Miami colors, another was a generic deep red that could've been from dozens of schools. They seemed enraptured by the panicked crush of people. Adam made sure they weren't looking and broke all rules by teleporting his avatar out of the packed streets. He appeared above Hammond for just a moment, then zipped to the apartment hallway, saving himself the walk. An elderly couple was staggering down the hall, clutching to one another. They gasped at the sudden presence of Adam, materializing out of nowhere. He ignored them and pounded on Belatrix's door.

"Bela, open up."

He heard something squeak inside the room, like a tight drawer being pushed shut.

"Who is it?"

"It's me. Open up."

The knob jumped; the door flew open. Belatrix stood there, hair veiling her face in loose wisps, her eyes wide.

"How did you get here so fast?" she asked.

Adam moved inside the apartment, his hands on her shoulders. She was trembling.

"I hurried right over."

"I just talked to you," she said. "You were at work."

Adam wasn't sure what his avatar had been doing before he arrived to borrow it. He rarely knew.

"I was already on my way. You called my portable, remember?"

Belatrix scrunched up her face, swiped the hair off her eyes and tucked it behind her ear. "I must be confused. It's— The world has gone nuts. What're we gonna do? What's *happening?*"

She looked toward the windows. Adam noticed the blinds had been drawn. Why was he lying to her about how he got to her apartment? What good did that do? Didn't he come there planning on telling her the truth? What good would *that* do? Was it better for her to go without knowing, to die thinking that she was real—?

Die. Why did he keep thinking about it like that? *Deleted*. She didn't exist. None of this was real. He had to fight to remind himself of that.

"Honey? Are you okay?" Belatrix put a hand on his chest, another around his waist. Adam realized he probably looked worse than she did. What was really about to happen to her planet was far more sinister, more permanent, more *real* than anything she could dread from the fake flying saucers.

"I have to tell you something," he said, even though he didn't yet know what he wanted to say.

There was an explosion outside; the windows rattled, then the vibrations could be felt in the floor. The building was swaying. Adam had never been on the ground level of a deletion before. It was terrifying and authentic. He couldn't believe how *real* it felt. Raw terror coursed up through him as he lost his center yet again. He had a brief pang of doubt that this world *was* real and that he was about to die. Perhaps his life at the university was some sort of delusion, and he really worked at Telematics Express on Hammond, selling accounts to—

Belatrix was screaming, her hands pressed to her cheeks. More rumbles of destruction sounded in the distance. Somewhere, avatars probably floated above it all, soaking up the data while their fleshy bodies sat in a room a billion virtual light years away. Adam's body was in that room as well. He tried to remember that.

"None of this is real!" he screamed, voicing his thoughts. The building moved again, or his balance was gone. He wasn't sure Belatrix heard him over her own screams. This was no way to say goodbye.

Belatrix's arms went out for balance. She looked around the room, eyes wide with a sudden look of concentration and desperation. "We have to go," she said. She hurried to her purse, dug around until she came out with her keys. She scanned the room for what else.

"It's no better anywhere else," Adam said. "There's something I have to say."

Anger flashed across her face. "Not now—" she began.

"None of this is real," Adam said again. He threw his arms wide and spun in a slow circle, accusing her entire world. "There are no aliens outside. There *is* no outside. This planet isn't real."

Belatrix dug out her phone and started dialing someone. She kept a wary eye on Adam. He realized how pointless and sad all this was, how impossible it would be to convince her with words, so he disappeared. He logged off, then reinserted himself near the ceiling of her apartment, teleporting as he had before. He lessened his personal gravity and drifted slowly toward the floor, his arms stretched wide and his knees bent. Belatrix dropped her phone. Her jaw hung agape.

"Sweetheart. Listen to me. I need you to know something." His feet reached the ground; Belatrix hadn't moved. "It's impossible to believe, I know. It's impossible to even explain, but this world is a virtual construct. It's an illusion created by my people on another planet—"

Her eyes darted toward the windows. Her lips and hands trembled.

"No." Adam stretched an arm toward the chaos outside. "I'm not with them. Those flying saucers aren't real either. It's—" He needed more time to explain. "Have you read about the simulations in the news? Did you know your world has created entire other virtual worlds? Computer systems have gone live recently where entire planets evolve and thrive so people can do research."

Belatrix nodded. "I've heard," she whispered. A lump rose and fell across her throat. She was terrified.

Adam pressed his palms toward the floor. "This is a world like that."

She shook her head. Fires crackled outside like paper being balled up and twisted. Adam could smell smoke.

"I know it's hard to imagine—" Adam waved at the room. "But all this is a simulation, just like the worlds your people have begun to create."

"But *you're* real." Her voice was a squeak. It was meant as a question. She didn't believe him.

"I'm real. And I came here because I need you to know that what we have between us—it's been the only thing in my life lately that's *felt* real."

Tears dripped from his chin, and Adam realized he was crying. He didn't know the simulation could do that. He didn't know why it wouldn't be able to, but he was surprised. Belatrix took a step toward him. Something in her face changed. Wide, disbelieving eyes had narrowed with suspicion. The teleportation trick, calling him at work and him showing up at her door, the absurdity of the scene outside the window, some internal doubts perhaps that had already been there—

"I'm ashamed of us in my world," Adam said, sobbing. "I'm living more of a lie than you are."

Belatrix reached out and held his arms. Her hands were shaking terribly. Tears were welling up in her own virtual eyes.

Adam wrapped her up. He could taste the salt of his tears on her neck. He wanted to take her with him, to teleport out and drag her back to reality, but she had no body there to inhabit even if such a thing were possible. A deeper part of him wanted something worse. It wanted to stay on Hammond, to die right then with her.

"I'm so sorry—" he said.

"Shhh."

She was comforting *him*.

The rumbles outside faded, leaving the wail of many distant, fearful screams.

"It's not fair," Adam whispered to no one.

"What's going to happen?" Belatrix asked.

He squeezed her tightly. "I wish I could save this—"

Adam wasn't sure if he meant the moment, her planet, Belatrix, or just the feeling of a better existence.

"What happens next?" she asked. "If you're right, if this isn't real, then what happens next?"

Adam went to kiss her, to feel the soft and warm sensation on his lips, as real as anything in the universe, one final time—

But there was no time.

His avatar automatically logged out as the planet he had been on ceased to exist.

7

> I am digital
> with the physical. And the
> other way around.

The interface room buzzed with human energy as Adam logged out. Laughter and chatter, the static of giddy elation, surrounded him and left little room for his dull sadness. Professors and researchers exchanged notes from their various and varied disaster scenes, the thrum of their enthusiasm drilling into Adam's head. He tugged his temple pads off the wires, then slowly peeled them from his head. He sat there, looking at them for a moment, then wiped the crust from his eyes. Samualson was still deeply interfaced beside him, his chin resting on his hands. His notepad of squiggly letters had grown over the last half hour. Adam wondered if his friend might have heard him yelling or crying as he repeatedly logged out to jot notes. He realized how little he cared, even if he had. He no longer wanted to hide Belatrix from his world; he wanted to share his memories of her.

Someone bumped into the back of Adam's chair, causing him to drop his temple pads. An apology was offered. Adam felt like killing the man. He felt like deleting something to make room in this world for Belatrix. He never felt anger like this, not this murderous rage. Such fury took more energy than he normally had. He suddenly felt a great reserve of it.

He stood and jostled his way through the joyousness, terrified by his own anger. A different crowd mingled outside. The thick glasses and rows of pocketed pens meant the planetary crowd was wasting no time forming a new world where Hammond had once been. There would be so much new empty space on the quantum drives. All those qubits were gone. The astronomers would get their accretion disc to mold a new world with. The joy on their faces, the anticipation, it reminded Adam of how he felt logging on each night. For them, the empty space around a star was like lover's lips to Adam. One man's heart was shattered to make whole dozens more. But these men could freely discuss their passion. There was no shame, no lie, nothing hidden. Adam remembered feeling that way about his literary discoveries once, long ago. He had had friends in the English department, people he drank coffee with, ate with. Now he had a girlfriend he'd never met and a love who had never existed. He wasn't yet forty and he might as well be dead.

He *felt* vaguely dead as he stumbled out the building and into the freshly fallen snow. Adam should have gone home. Distantly, he knew that. He hadn't slept in two nights. He went to the cafeteria instead and drank coffee. The taste and the heat of it felt far removed from him. He listened to the clamor from the kitchen, the rattle of plastic trays and clang of silverware and chatter from the night crew. He watched the cashier flip slowly through her romance novel, scratching her head through her hairnet now and then. Through frosted glass, he could see a veil of snow begin to descend on campus. He wondered if there would be enough to cancel his morning class. Somehow, he knew he wouldn't be teaching that day even if they didn't call it off. He was going to be sick. He already was sick.

He nursed his coffee until the last sip was cold, went to grab his backpack and realized he'd left it in the lab. He'd left his gloves in there as well. He had his jacket, but couldn't remember putting it on. The analog clock on the wall let him know he'd been spacing out for hours. A group in lab coats sat in a booth across from him, gesturing excitedly for the late hour. Adam didn't remember them coming in. He wondered if he'd slept. It would be nice if he had.

He went back out into the cold. The snow was the wet kind, sticking to his hair. Adam pulled his hood up and thought briefly about heading back to the lab, then realized he didn't care about the backpack. He trudged up the walk toward the library—another of the sleepless buildings on campus. He knew all the sleepless buildings well.

The policeman behind the night desk waved in recognition. Adam dipped his head. He sank into a chair by the periodicals and tried to sleep. He gave up as the sun eventually peeked over the mountains and the students began to emerge from their dorm caves.

The snow had ceased; it wasn't enough to close campus. Adam knew he needed to call the department secretary, let her know he wouldn't be coming to class, but even that required some semblance of motivation. He needed an excuse to not call in sick. He wasn't well enough for even that.

The long walk to his apartment was chewed up one lumbering step at a time. Up several walkways, around the education building, up, up, up more steps. He pushed down on his knees to force them to work. The snow to either side seemed inviting. Adam imagined spreading out on the wide blanket of it, letting the cold erode away the last of sensation. He would sleep forever and never wake, never feel. He willed himself to do it, could *feel* his insides moving that way, but the shell of him kept staggering forward and up the steps, taking the rest of him home with it.

He could barely feel the keys in his numb fingers. He couldn't tell the door was already unlocked as he worked it open. Adam was too far gone to notice the puddles on the linoleum as he crossed the foyer and into his living room. It was several moments, even, before he realized someone was sitting at his computer.

"Hello?"

A woman spun around, a worried frown breaking into a brief smile, then back to the worried frown.

"Hello, Adam."

He didn't know this woman. Was this his landlord's wife? He tried to think who would have a key, or a reason to be here. Why would she be on his computer? Adam needed sleep.

"I'm Amanda."

The woman rose from the chair and took a step toward him. Adam was too tired to recoil. If she hadn't been standing by his computer, the name wouldn't have registered as one he knew. With the computer in the background, though, it made sense.

"Amanda?"

This was his girlfriend, the one he chatted nightly with, his *virtual* girlfriend. She nodded.

"Are you okay?" She touched her own face while gazing at Adam's. She looked worried. Everyone gave him that worried look of late.

"I haven't slept," Adam said. "What are you doing here?" He was simply curious. He strangely didn't care, couldn't quite manage it.

Amanda looked around the apartment. Adam saw the clutter through her eyes. He noticed the tall piles of debris had been raked flat, like fall leaves pushed back to their former state. A dim awareness told him Amanda had been going through his things. He almost cared.

"I thought you had an early class," she said.

"But why?" He shook his head, clearing the cobwebs. "You've been here before? How do you even know where I live?"

"I'm sorry about this." She waved her hands at the room. "But I couldn't wait. I couldn't."

Adam held up his hands. "I need sleep," he said. "I can't handle this right now. I can't even begin to think about it. I've been up three days straight."

He staggered toward the bedroom. He didn't care that his online girlfriend was in his house. It almost felt natural. *Inevitable.* Some part of him processed that she was prettier than he'd imagined she'd be, but even that couldn't douse the growing surety that he no longer wanted her as a part of his life.

Amanda followed after him. "Adam, I need your writings."

"My what?" He mumbled it to himself as he reached the bedroom door.

"Your writings. All of them. I need them now."

Adam leaned on the knob. His head was throbbing. He shook it, and the entire planet seemed to wobble around him. "You need them now."

"Right now. I'm sorry to have to ask, but I can't find them."

Adam turned away from the door and scanned the room. He glanced at the old computer. "They're not there." He waved at his head. "They're in here."

Amanda visibly wilted. She looked at her watch. "How many haiku haven't I heard?"

"I can't do this," Adam said. "I need you to leave. You shouldn't have come here."

She didn't look all that upset to hear this. She took a step toward him.

"Did you hear about Virginia Tech?" she asked him.

He remembered something about Virginia Tech. He couldn't quite place it.

"Their servers," Amanda said.

Adam nodded. "Yeah," he said. He remembered Samualson saying something. None of this made sense. He just wanted to sleep.

"Tech has already duped the data from M.I.T. to their own servers. They have a dozen worlds already up and running this morning. Dozens more are coming online at universities all over the world." Amanda frowned. "Did you know your South Korea went online with their own virtual world last week?"

"*My* South Korea?" Adam fell sideways against the

doorjamb and remained propped there. He was going to fall asleep standing up.

"I can't keep taking them down, Adam." Amanda looked grave. "It takes too much time. More are going up faster than I can take them down. My boss won't have any more of it, not for the trickle coming out of this planet." She waved her hands around her.

Adam pressed his palms to his sore temples. One girlfriend was deleted, the other was crazy. He slid down the wall until his ass hit the carpet. His head rested in his hands.

"I need anything you can give me," Amanda said. He heard her cross the room, could feel her standing above him. "Three or four haiku. Anything. Please, I wish we had more time."

"Tomorrow," Adam said. "Please leave me alone."

A hand clamped down on his wrist. "There *is* no tomorrow," Amanda hissed. He looked up at her. "Are you listening to me? I know what you do, who you are. I'm a plagiarist too, Adam. You know how this works; I don't have time to explain it to you." Amanda pointed toward his window. "You've got hours left. Your legacy is all that matters. Don't you understand?" She shook her head. "Of course you don't. You have no idea what you mean on my world. You don't know what I've discovered in you."

Amanda stepped away from him. Adam felt bile rise up in his throat. Her words were settling like snow upon his consciousness, forming something like understanding.

"What are you saying?" Adam asked. He looked at his palms, flexed his fingers.

"Please," she said. She backed away from him and looked out the window. The blinds were up. Adam never had the blinds up. "A few haiku. You have to say them to me. I can't copy it straight out of your mind. You know how it works."

"This is *real*," Adam told himself. What she was saying seemed so familiar. He rubbed his fingers together. It felt as real as the sims.

It felt as real as the sims.

"I'm sorry," Amanda said, not for the first time. "I really am. I like you. I— I feel maybe more than I should for you." She bit her lip and looked away. "This isn't easy for me—"

"This is *real*," Adam repeated. He stood up and took a step toward Amanda. Outside, the sun was peeking over the mountains, the clear sky dazzling against the fresh snow. The brightness of it lanced into Adam's brain.

"Say whatever comes to mind," Amanda said. "You'll be remembered for it."

"I'll be remembered," he whispered.

"Yes."

But Belatrix won't be, he realized. It was what he'd wanted to tell her, but couldn't find the words. She was real as long as he'd known her, and would *remain* real as long as he could recall her. Belatrix was as real as anyone he'd known who was now lost. As real as anyone who had become ash, leaving just memories behind with the living. She was as real as his father had been to him. Had his father been real? Was Adam real? Was this some kind of trick? If he was deleted, and the memory of Belatrix was deleted with him, then she was lost for good. His mind spun with the layers and layers and layers: Hammond had started simming their own worlds, placing a strain on the campus computers, so it had to be deleted. What about all those simmed worlds on Hammond when that happened? Adam had considered the loss of Belatrix, of the world and people she knew, but what about the billions of others residing on computers another layer deep? Those people thought they were real. What had they been doing when they were deleted? How few were told in advance?

Adam looked out over campus, at the amazing view from his window that he'd seen maybe once or twice before.

"How long?" he asked. He thought about the hundreds of worlds simmed on Earth. How many had worlds simming in them? Or in *them*, one more layer deep? How many Earths were there on Amanda's world? Could this be real?

"Not much time," she said.

"What if *you're* not real," Adam said. He pressed his hand against the frosted glass and felt the cold beyond.

"I think about that a lot," she told him.

Adam wanted her to not be real. He wanted company in that sudden loneliness that had overtaken him. He wanted to hurt her in some way.

"These things happen so fast," she said. "They reach a tipping point before we see it coming. Believe me, I did everything I could—"

"You were the one razing our farms," he said.

The accusation frosted on the glass by his hand.

"I tried everything I could—"

"Make a copy." Adam turned to her. "Make a copy of me. Or delete more farms." Real or not, he didn't want to cease existing. He felt a surge of panic. Adam looked back over the roofs of the department buildings. "I can pull the plug on our servers. I can. I know where the backup relays are. It'll make some room on your own servers—"

Amanda placed a hand on his shoulder. "Adam, it's been decided much higher up than me. I've already begged on your behalf."

"On my behalf?" He wiped tears from his cheeks. "What do you mean? I'm nothing."

Amanda frowned. Her eyes were following his tears as they streamed down. She seemed reluctant to touch him any further.

"That's not true," she said. She bit her lip again. "We are drowning in stuff to consume, just like you, just like *all* the words that are simmed and the worlds *they* sim. But I found your poetry, this limited syllabic form found nowhere else, this simplicity, this elegance constrained. I've become an expert on it, on haiku. I've mined the ancient hills of Earth for every nugget. I've combed the books and scrolls and tablets, going back to its Eastern roots—but you are the one."

Adam sobbed. His head spun from the night's tragedy and the day's disbelief.

Amanda touched his cheek.

"The hours we spend pouring over a single poem of yours—" Amanda sighed. "They are the closest we get to silence on my world. The closest to a pause for thought. We sip on your works, Adam Griffey, to keep from drowning in all else."

"That can't be true," he said. The sobs and tears felt so *real*.

"The end is coming any moment now," Amanda said. "Please don't take them with you. Please."

Adam swiped at his cheeks. He was about to speak when there was a great rumble outside. It seemed to emanate from the very belly of the Earth. Amanda looked past him to the window. Adam turned. A plume of dark smoke burst up through the milky white of a hillside. Mountains, long dormant, erupted. A cone of black mixed with bright red, fading as it coursed through the cold air. The ground spit dirt. Crimson rivers leaked like wounds from the Earth. The world shook. Amanda pleaded.

"The world that isn't," Adam said, "becomes simply that once more." He pressed both palms to the glass. He felt Amanda's arms around him. He lost himself between the cold and the warm.

"And all is gray ash," he concluded.

Also by Hugh Howey

Molly Fyde and the Parsona Rescue
Molly Fyde and the Land of Light
Molly Fyde and the Blood of Billions
Molly Fyde and the Fight for Peace

Half Way Home

About the Author

Hugh Howey is the author of the award winning Molly Fyde series. After spending much of his life at sea, he finally settled down in the mountains of Boone, North Carolina where he lives with his wife, Amber, and his dog. When he isn't writing, he can be found at the Appalachian State University Bookstore or taking the occasional class and pestering the occasional professor.

Made in the USA
San Bernardino, CA
06 May 2014